A CHERRY TO DIE FOR

DOG DETECTIVES - THE BEAGLE MYSTERIES

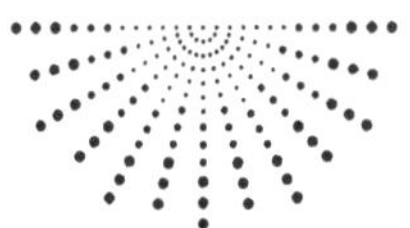

ROSIE SAMS

AGATHA PARKER

SWEETBOOKHUB.COM

Welcome to our new book. We hope you enjoy this wonderful series of cozy mystery books all featuring a sweet little Beagle puppy. Mazie is an ex-police dog who was wounded in service. She is gifted to Hannah Barry, a broken-hearted realtor who is down on her luck.

At first, Hannah is unsure, can she learn to love the Beagle? What will she do when a body is found?

If you missed it, find out how Mazie found a new home, and Hannah some peace, in this fabulous box set of the first 6 books in this much loved series.

Dog Detective – The Beagle Mysteries Book 1 to 6

Rosie has a free book Smudge and the Stolen Puppies that you can pick up. It is about an amazing and cute French Bulldog the best Dog Detective in all of Port Warren. Grab it here for FREE

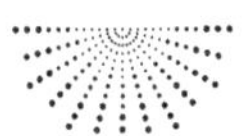

Hannah Barry tucked her blonde hair behind her ears as she sorted through her files. She was a private investigator in a small town in Vermont, Blairstown. When she was involved in a case, she spent all her energy on it, and between cases, she liked to organize the paperwork fallout. Today was one of those days. She'd fortified herself with a strong, black coffee, and her trusty sidekick, Mazie. The former police dog was a tri-colored beagle who'd helped her get through many cases to date and Hannah loved that she was as good at keeping her company during filing as she was investigating a crime scene.

As she flipped through her notes from various cases, Hannah recalled the details from the cases. When she made it to her most recent case which involved a bride who left the alter for the lead singer in the wedding band, she smiled at the memory, happy that things worked out for the best. Then her mind moved to something her boyfriend, Colin Troughton, had said to her when they were discussing the case a few weeks later.

"Going slow is wise at times, but I also think that taking the leap when the moment feels right is also wise."

Her hands paused as she recalled his words. They'd been confusing to her at the time. She hadn't addressed it in the moment, nor brought it up after the fact; nevertheless, his statement had stuck with her. She took a moment to ponder the meaning again, before busying herself with filing her paperwork. Mazie snoozed on a dog bed in the corner, and she took another sip of coffee. She could do it.

Mercifully, she was interrupted by a knock on her office door. She looked up to see who it was, thrilled for the distraction. "Anita!" she announced. "I'm so happy to see you." Hannah jumped to her feet to greet her friend with a hug.

Anita laughed. "Wow. Hi, Hannah." She glanced around the room. "Everything going okay in here?"

"Yes. Everything is fine, I'm just filing paperwork. You know how much I love that."

"Ah." Anita nodded in understanding. "I hear you. The administration is the worst part." Anita Gomez owned the local coffee shop, Jolt of Java, with her husband, Oscar. Lucky for Hannah, it was located right down the street from her office.

Mazie's keen hound nose stuck in the air and began sniffing. Anita moved over to scratch the dog behind her ears. "You have a great nose, Mazie! I brought over some new treats that I've been working on." She juggled the paper bag she'd been carrying in front of Mazie, who sat obediently, waiting for a taste of the goodies.

"What have you been working on?" Hannah asked.

"I have some pumpkin biscotti here."

"Oh, I'd love to try some," Hannah exclaimed.

Anita shook her head. "They look delicious, and they are delicious... but for animals. I've made them specifically for the pets who come into the shop," she said.

"Genius!" Hannah replied. "That's why you and Oscar are so great at what you do. You run that place with such love, the customers can feel it."

"Oh, Hannah. You're sweet," Anita said. "But let's not get ahead of ourselves. Let's see what Mazie thinks first." She fed Mazie a piece of biscotti and they both watched to see her reaction. They didn't have to watch for long because Mazie scarfed it down and looked back at Anita expectantly, sitting and waiting for another piece.

Anita clapped her hands in delight. "You like them!"

"I'd say she more than likes them!" Hannah said. She moved back to her desk and spun her chair back and forth while staring into the distance.

"Um, Hannah? Anything I can help you with?" Anita asked.

"What?" Hannah asked, jerking to alert. "Oh, no. I'm fine."

"You're not fine," Anita replied, sitting on the desk to face her friend, folding her arms across her chest. "Spill it."

Hannah sighed. "Okay. You're right. I've been thinking a lot about something Colin said a while ago."

Anita cocked her head to the side. "Oh?"

"Yeah. He mentioned that sometimes taking a leap is appropriate when the moment feels right."

Anita waited. When Hannah didn't elaborate, she replied. "Wait, so you're worried that he's – what, really interested in you?"

Hannah gave her a small smile. "I know it sounds crazy, but I have this suspicion that Colin is going to propose at any moment."

"I'm still not seeing the issue, Hannah!" Anita said. "In fact, since you brought it up, this is amazing news! If you ask me, it's high time you and Colin got hitched." Her face brightened to a giant grin.

"I know. I'm sorry, I'm not communicating my concerns well. I'm excited about the prospect, but my issue is with the expectations that are building. He hasn't said anything more than that mention of taking a leap, and now I have my hopes set high on the fact that we'll be getting engaged. That can't be healthy! It's taking up so much of my mental energy. What if I'm reading it wrong, how am I going to deal with the disappointment?"

"I see," Anita replied, her face creasing in sympathy. "Try to stay hopeful. We all know how much Colin adores you. I'm sure things will work out as they should."

Hannah gave her friend a little pout. "Okay. You're right. I'll try to keep a smile on my face, with my fingers crossed."

Hannah's office phone rang just in time to transition Hannah out of her pity party. "Hannah Barry, P.I." Hannah listened and took notes for a few moments while the person on the other end of the phone spoke. "Hmm. I see. Okay. I understand. Yes, that could work. Right, great idea. I suppose we could make that happen. All right, Ms. Moriarty. I'll keep you posted." Hannah hung the phone up and looked at her friend.

Anita watched in amusement. "What did Ellen have to say? Does she want to plan a party for you?" Ellen Moriarty was a local party planner.

Shaking her head, Hannah filled her in on the details. "Ellen thinks that her soon-to-be ex-husband is trying to poach her clients."

Anita's eyebrows raised in interest. "Seth, her almost ex, and business partner?"

"That's the one," Hannah confirmed. "Ellen wants me to perform a stake out at a party Seth is hosting soon. She thinks he's hosting an exclusive event for Wendy Hill."

"Who's Wendy?" Anita asked.

"She's a local girl who's rumored to be announcing her upcoming engagement to a New York financier, Tyler Callahan, soon," Hannah replied. "Ellen said that she'd supposedly landed the party, but evidently never heard back from Wendy, and now she suspects that Seth has swooped in."

"Interesting. Maybe not a crime, but not a great move," Anita said.

"Right, I agree. It sounds like more of a personal matter to me, honestly. But Ellen sounded really upset, almost pleading, really. She suggested that I just go to the party to check things out."

"And how will you do that? Won't Seth recognize you?" Anita asked.

"Seth won't know who I am, and he'll be so busy with the details, but funny enough, Ellen did suggest that I don a costume, just in case."

Anita released a laugh. "A costume? Like, a disguise? What does she have in mind, a fake nose and mustache attached to some glasses for you to wear?"

Hannah chuckled in reply. "I probably won't take it that far, but I did agree to go. Would you and Oscar like to join us as we scope out the scene?"

Mazie began barking, likely because she wanted more biscotti, but the timing made the women laugh. "Sounds like Mazie thinks we should," Anita said.

"Then it's a plan. We're going on a double date to the big party!" Hannah replied.

CHAPTER TWO

*L*ater that evening, Hannah had finally filed away the last of her most recent cases and opened a fresh folder for the new one. With a sharpie, she labeled it, "Moriarty". She wiped her hands together and placed the marker back in the drawer. "There we go," she whispered. She stood up and whistled to Mazie. "Shall we head over to Troughton's Trough?"

Mazie scampered to her feet and ran to the door, sitting patiently while Hannah made her way over. The two of them walked just next door to Colin's restaurant. It was just before the dinner rush, so Hannah knew they'd be able to grab a quick bite to eat together before the madness began.

When they entered the restaurant, Colin was shining the glassware on the white linen-covered tables. He looked up when the door opened. "Hannah, Mazie!" He took swift steps across the room to embrace Hannah. "Come on, I have the chef preparing something for us." He ushered them to a table in the corner. Colin poured Hannah a splash of red wine. "I'm guessing you need this after a day of organizing," he said.

"Oh, thank you. You know me so well!" she said, closing her eyes, anticipating the trickle down her throat. "You're right. It was a day, but I do feel great about having it all finished!"

"Cheers to that," he said. "Anything interesting happen today? Other than a papercut or two?"

"Actually, there was a new case," Hannah said.

"Do tell," Colin said, leaning back in his chair. Colin was nothing if not supportive of Hannah's career. He was the one who originally encouraged her to leave her job as a realtor to pursue more formal work as a private investigator. Since then, he'd happily come along to help her investigate whenever he could.

Hannah was happy to oblige. "You know Ellen Moriarty?"

"The party planner?"

'Yes. Well, she and her ex-husband, Seth, are still untangling their joint business together. She called me to go undercover at his next party to see if he stole her client or not." Hannah had a glint in her eye as she mentioned it.

"Stole her client, huh? And is that a crime?"

"Not at all, but she was very persistent about it. I figured it wouldn't hurt anything to take the case. In fact, the first order of business is to infiltrate an engagement party. I'm to show up in a disguise and everything!" she said

Colin laughed at the news. "Please, tell me I'll be able to join you?"

"Yes, but only if you agree to wear a disguise," she smiled.

"Done," he said, placing his hands on the table. "I'll start planning now."

Hannah rolled her eyes. "An engagement party should be a time for happiness, free of intrigue."

Colin held her eye contact for a beat longer than usual and she felt her cheeks warm. There they were dancing around the subject of marriage again. He stood up and walked to her side of the table. "It's time for me to get back to work, but I need this to get me through." He held his hands out for her to grab them and helped her to her feet. He scooped Hannah into his arms and kissed his girlfriend until Mazie began barking at their feet. They both laughed as he loosened his grip on her. Then he furrowed his brow. "Are you going to find a disguise for Mazie?"

Hannah smirked. "In fact," she said, reaching for her phone. She began scrolling through social media until she found what she was looking for. She showed it to Colin, pointing out that the venue's host, Priscilla Ralston, is known for letting guests bring their pets to her restaurant.

Colin studied the photos. "Animals in her restaurant? But why?" Hannah knew the idea of animals roaming his fine dining establishment would be a logistical night-mare for him.

"She likes the pets to sample her savory treats in the outdoor area. It's like her thing. People book with her specifically for the entertainment and convenience of it.

The guests enjoy their interior accommodations while the pets have a night out as well."

Colin smiled and scratched the top of Mazie's head. "Well, that's perfect, then, isn't it, Mazie? You'll have a great time, and you're bound to make some new friends."

"Mazie will make some new friends, sure, but that's about all I can see coming from the night," Hannah said skeptically.

"At the very least, we'll enjoy a fine meal," Colin offered.

"True. We'll have a fun night. The biggest mystery will be me finding a way to tell Ellen that poaching clients isn't a crime."

CHAPTER THREE

A few nights later, Colin and Hannah met up with Oscar and Anita outside Priscilla's Place. Hannah had decided not to sneak into the actual party, but to reserve a small table just outside the private dining area where the party was held. That way everyone could attend costume-free, and still observe the party at close proximity. She did decide, however, to put Mazie in the "puppy playpen" just for the experience of it.

The foursome took their seats and ordered drinks to start, Hannah positioned to face the party. The private area had glass windows for her to casually peek into. Just after the waiter brought their drinks, the engagement party began spilling out into the main dining area. *What's this?* Hannah thought.

"Hannah, are you seeing anything interesting?" Oscar asked.

"Shh." Hannah placed an index finger over her mouth. "I need to listen to everything. This is prime time!" She tuned everyone at her table out as she watched Wendy Hill, the local girl who'd caught Tyler Callahan's eye, argue with her fiancé, Tyler. Her long, wavy red hair fell around her shoulders and her green eyes were laser-focused on her man. She could definitely confirm that Seth was, in fact, hosting the engagement party for the couple. Case closed; he stole his ex-wife's client. Despite the case being closed, she was intrigued. What were they arguing about? She angled her ear towards the argument.

Tyler's sister, Krystle, stood with her hands on her hips. Her short blonde hair was recently highlighted and her clear brown eyes were staring into Wendy. Beside Krystle stood Wendy's future father-in-law, Drake. He was the spitting image of Krystle with the same blond hair and brown eyes. He was a tall, imposing man and he wore a frown. "You're just a gold-digging opportunist!" Krystle said.

"We know what you're doing," Drake added. "The Callahan family has a very particular nose for those whose motives aren't pure."

Wendy looked aghast.

A waitress came over with drinks and handed them to Drake Callahan. Drake examined the pink-tinged champagne cocktail with a cherry in it. "What's this?" he spit angrily.

The waitress looked shaken. "Your drink, sir."

"This is not what I ordered. What is this cherry doing in here? What kind of service is this?" He looked to Wendy. "You can't even plan a party right!"

At this, tears began rolling down Wendy's cheek. "I never asked for this celebration! I never asked to marry a Callahan. I didn't ask for any of this!" she cried.

Seth Moriarty had been in the private dining area and had missed the disturbance, but when he came out, he made eye contact with Hannah. He moved to their table. "Hello, everyone. I hope you're enjoying your evening," he said.

"A lovely event, thank you," Colin said.

"Indeed, you've done a lovely job," Hannah agreed. Seth gave a satisfied smile as he surveyed the room. Then Hannah continued. "I heard Ellen was supposed to plan this party, are you two working together again?" She was relieved that everyone at the table held their neutral faces in light of her little fib.

In response, Seth shoved his hands in his pockets and looked from left to right, unable to make eye contact. "Enjoy the night," he mumbled before taking a hasty leave towards two men at the bar who were raising their voices to one another.

Meanwhile, Priscilla Ralston appeared from the kitchen. Her long black hair contrasted with her green eyes as she scanned the room. She clapped her hands to get the attention of the guests. "Please, everyone. Let's make our way back to the private dining area where we can better serve you all!" she said, casting a worried glance at the patrons attempting to enjoy their meal in the regular dining area.

The guests seemed not to notice her when Hanna's attention was turned back to Wendy. Now she was standing with her fiancé, Tyler.

"Why can't you just stand up for me?" she asked, her voice strained. "I need a supportive partner, not someone who's going to let his family speak to me that way." She was begging him, and he stood expressionless watching his father.

Hannah noticed that Drake had become increasingly more intoxicated over the short time she'd been observing him. He had made up for the erroneous drink the waitress brought him by replacing it with multiple whiskey shots. Tyler cast a nervous eye in the direction of his dad. Hannah thought Tyler seemed scared of Drake, and she couldn't blame him for it.

With Tyler's lackluster response, Wendy threw her hands in the air. "Forget it!" she said before rushing off.

Hannah exchanged a quick look with Colin before she followed the direction of the ill-fated bride-to-be. On the way out, Hannah passed the doggy playpen and scooped Mazie out of there. The two of them exited Priscilla's Place in search of Wendy. It took only moments to locate the poor woman. Hannah simply had to follow the sounds of her crying.

Mazie scampered over to the woman, nuzzling her legs in comfort. Hannah wasn't far behind. "Are you okay, Wendy?" she asked in a soothing voice, kneeling next to her.

Wendy lifted her tear-stained face from her hands to meet Hannah's imploring gaze. "I know I'm of a lower class. I know I'm not what the Callahans are used to, but I believed that Tyler could convince his family that my heart is true. That I'm worth it." She released a quiet sob. "I'm so ashamed of what I thought about him tonight. I watched as he was silent in response to the vitriol his sister and father were spewing, and all I could think about was what a coward he is." She was quiet for a moment, breathing hard. "His response, I don't know. His failure to come to my defense makes me wonder if our marriage will ever be a sure thing."

Hannah nodded in sympathy. "I'm so sorry, Wendy. You deserve much better than that. I don't know Tyler, but I know you're worth it. It's hard standing up to our families, maybe he was having a bad day?" Hannah didn't believe that herself, but she wanted the woman to feel better.

"Everything was fine between me and Tyler. More than fine. We were madly in love without a care in the world. That is until Krystle and Drake showed up. I feel like Tyler changed completely when they came to town. If this is the real him, I can't be married to him," Wendy said. She buried her head in her hands again.

Hannah reached her arm around the crying girl when she abruptly stood up. "I just want to be alone," she said. "I need time to think." Hannah watched as she ducked behind the restaurant, just as Colin came out in search of her.

"Hey, Hannah!" he called. Mazie barked in reply. "Over here!"

He sat next to her and pulled her in closer to himself. "So, is the case closed?

"While we confirmed that Seth is certainly shady, I also found out that Wendy and Tyler's engagement seems unlikely to last."

Colin breathed in through his teeth. "Ouch."

"I know. Beyond that, though, there is no real crime to speak of."

Colin sighed. "I'm sorry. Does all of this turn you off of the idea of engagements entirely?" he asked in a quiet voice.

Slowly, Hannah shook her head. Colin took her hand and held it between his own. "Good," he said and reached to kiss her cheek. Then he reached into his pocket. Hannah's heart began hammering in her chest. This was it; he was going to propose. She held her breath and tried to suppress her smile when a sharp cry rang out from the back of the venue.

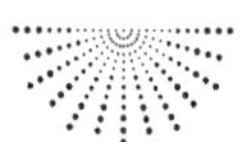

CHAPTER FOUR

Hannah and Colin pulled away from one another and met each other's startled glances. Mazie barked and they all moved together towards the source of the cry. They raced around the back of Priscilla's Place and found a body lying still in the alley. It was a large, imposing body, with a full head of blond hair.

"Drake Callahan!" Hannah yelled, racing to his side. Then she skidded to a stop when another figure, previously hidden by the darkness, revealed itself. It was a woman with wavy, red hair. Hannah wasn't sure what registered first, that it was Wendy Hill lurking in the shadows, or that she was holding a bloody block of wood in her hand.

Mazie began circling in distress, barking as she went. She scratched wildly at the dumpster, sniffing the perimeter of it. Hannah heard footsteps behind her. She turned to see that some of the other guests were spilling out the back of the restaurant and had formed a crowd. They called back inside the restaurant for others to come to observe the scene and things devolved quickly into chaos.

Finally, Krystle came running out of the establishment and pushed her way to the front of the crowd. A hush came over the people around her as soon as they realized that it was the victim's daughter elbowing her way through. She looked down at the heap of her father's body, then back to Wendy. She was silent, likely in shock as the death of her father registered with her. Then she very slowly trained her gaze back on Wendy and her eyes hardened. "You're holding the weapon," she said in a low, controlled voice.

As if surprised by this pronouncement, Wendy looked to the bloody piece of wood in her hand and jerked back in shock.

"You're holding a bloody piece of wood, with my father's blood on it!" she cried. "Look!" She pointed to the injury dotting her father's brow. "Arrest her!" she called out to no one in particular, but loud enough for everyone to hear. "Wendy Hill has murdered my father. Police! Help!"

Wendy suddenly unfroze. She dropped the piece of wood and took a step away, attempting to distance herself from both the weapon and the scene itself. "It wasn't me; I swear it!"

Krystle folded her arms across her chest. "Caught red-handed, is that what they say? There isn't much you can say that would convince anyone otherwise."

"No, I swear it. I came back here for some space to think. I saw this piece of wood laying in the middle of the alleyway and picked it up to investigate. In the dark, the blood looked like paint. I was wondering if it was part of some art installation."

Krystle audibly scoffed. "Listen to this creative liar!"

"I'm serious! Then, around the corner, I saw your father, laying here, already dead!" She glanced frantically around the crowd in search of Tyler. He had slowly made his way through the crowd and was standing at the front of everyone, taking in the scene with shock. His eyes looked empty, but when Wendy found him, they softened slightly.

"Tyler!" she cried in relief. "Tell your sister I'm not capable of murder. Tell her I'd never do such a thing!"

He said nothing, but he shook his head slowly and pursed his lips. He glanced between Wendy and Krystle, obviously pained about the choice he was being asked to make. Lucky for him the sound of police sirens rang out over the crowd, and everyone collectively turned to see them approach the group. Their blue and red lights twisted in the night sky, casting a colorful shadow over the faces in the crowd.

Hannah watched as the blonde hair of Kate Carver, the local police chief, ran to the scene of the crime, the observers parting to make way. Ralph, her stocky deputy followed behind her. "All right, folks. The show is over. Back it up, back it up," Ralph said, stretching his arms wide and moving the crowd further away from Drake's body.

Kate moved directly to Hannah for a quick recap. "What's going on here?" she asked quietly.

"Wendy here claims she happened upon this body."

"Do you know the victim?" Kate asked.

"Yes. It's Drake Callahan." Hannah hesitated for a split second before moving closer to Kate and lowering her voice. "It's Wendy's future father-in-law."

Kate turned to Hannah with her eyes wide and knowing. "I see. Thank you." She moved to Wendy's side. "Let's have a seat over here," she said, noting the young woman's pale pallor and shallow breaths. "I'd like to ask you a few questions about what went on tonight."

Wendy nodded and gulped. "Okay," she whispered.

After a very quick interaction, Kate stood up and nodded to Ralph. Ralph swiftly moved to Kate's side and removed his handcuffs from his belt.

"Ms. Hill, I'm sorry to say this, but we have to place you under arrest," Kate said. "You are under suspicion for the murder of Drake Callahan," Kate said the words simply, but Hannah heard the sadness in her tone.

"What?" Wendy's voice suddenly found its volume. "I didn't do this! You can't arrest me!" she shouted. "I wouldn't kill anyone, please, please!" she pleaded, scanning around again for her fiancé, who by this point was nowhere to be found.

Hannah looped her hand through Colin's waiting as they watched the scene carry itself to the police cruisers. "I guess the case just opened back up?" Colin asked.

"Ha! You can say that again," Hannah replied.

Colin seemed to move back and forth. "Nice night, isn't it?" he asked, looking to the stars. Admittedly, they were putting on a spectacular show that evening, but Hannah was having trouble enjoying it with everything else going on.

"It's beautiful, yes," she said. The thought crossed her mind that Colin was acting a little bit strange, but she had more pressing concerns at the moment. "Let's go into the restaurant to see what people are saying in there."

Colin nodded wordlessly and the two of them made their way back inside. He cast a forlorn glance back to the sky just as they crossed the threshold to the restaurant. "Hannah, I..."

Hannah stopped to see what he had to say. Then he shook his head. "Never mind. Let's head in."

When they walked into the room, Hannah noticed Tyler speaking in hushed tones with his sister, just next to the kitchen. She and Colin maneuvered closer to them so they could overhear what was being said.

Meanwhile, Seth was wide-eyed and panicked as he hovered around Krystle, pacing around nervously. Hannah thought it was odd that he was waiting so close to her rather than trying to save the rest of the party. Then as if something snapped in Krystle, she turned to Seth and snarled at him. Hannah wasn't yet close enough to hear what she said, but Seth's head jerked back in surprise. He ducked his head down and backed away, muttering his apologies.

Hannah watched as he made his way back to the kitchen, thinking that Seth must know more than what he was saying. She had some investigating to do, and she thought there was no better person to start with than the event planner himself.

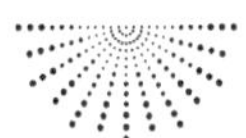

"*L*et's go find out what that was all about," Hannah said to Colin. Mazie barked and hopped around at her feet as if approving of Hannah's plan. She looked to Colin to see his reaction, and she was sure she caught his face sag for just a split second before he recovered.

"Great idea let's do it," he replied.

She took a single step then stopped. "Colin, was there something you wanted to say to me?" she asked him.

He looked down at her with his clear green eyes and paused, his eyes scanning her face. Then he sighed as Mazie barked again. He shook his head. "Nothing important. Let's go see what Seth has to say."

Hannah was a woman on a mission and turned resolutely back to face Tyler and Krystle. Even still, she couldn't help but feel her heart weigh heavily in her chest as Colin shook his head. She wondered if Colin ever intended to propose, or again if it was all in her head. Even she had to admit that a proposal at a crime scene wouldn't have been the most romantic thing, but then again, given their crime-solving together, maybe it would have been perfect? She shook her head. She was overanalyzing things, yet again.

Hannah, Colin, and Mazie made their way into the kitchen where they'd seen Seth go.

When they walked in, they saw him deep in conversation with Priscilla. Priscilla looked concerned and serious as they spoke, and when Hannah and Colin walked in, she glanced up, relief washing over her face as she registered who it was. "I'll leave you all to talk," she said, stepping aside to leave them alone.

Seth, meanwhile, hadn't looked up. He was pacing around, muttering to himself. "I thought I could do it. I took too much on. I wanted to prove I could do this and now, look at me."

"Um, Seth?" Hannah said, placing a gentle hand on his back. "Everything okay?"

His face swiveled to meet hers. "Everything okay? Hannah, have you not been here all evening? I've just thrown my first ever party without the help of Ellen, and someone was murdered!"

Hannah nodded. "Yes, I'm aware of that, of course. I meant, is everything okay with you. You seem very stressed."

He looked at her incredulously. "Yes, yes, Hannah. I'm stressed. To say the very least."

"Are we able to help with anything?" Hannah cast an exasperated look at Colin as if asking for his assistance with the unreasonable party planner.

Seth finally stopped pacing and ran a hand through his hair. "Listen, I was trying to prove I could do this without Ellen. I thought I didn't need her, for parties, or my life. But all this night has done has made me realize that I can't do it without her. I can't do anything without her!" he said.

"Oh," realization hit Hannah. This was not what she expected him to say.

"Not to mention the fact that she'll likely take me to the cleaners in our upcoming divorce. She's going to take everything from me!"

"I thought the two of you were already divorced," Hannah said.

"We've been separated, but the final paperwork is pending. I know she's going to take so much of my money, and I was trying this party out to see if I could make it work without her. But now I know that it only worked *with* her!" Hannah watched as the man verbally processed not just the disaster of an evening, but his whole life with the woman he once loved. Sadness came over her.

"Oh, Seth. I'm so sorry. This seems like something Ellen might want to hear, though. I wonder if there isn't still a chance for you two to work things out?"

Seth was quiet then as if considering what Hannah had to say. Then she used the opportunity to steer the subject to the murder. "So, Seth. What happened tonight, do you know? I left to follow Wendy outside when she got upset with Tyler and was wondering what took place in the restaurant in my absence."

Seth looked to the ceiling and rolled his eyes. "Honestly, what didn't happen tonight. After the two of you left, I ran after Krystle who was equally upset about the argument, and she ends up throwing her wine glass in her upset. Meanwhile, Tyler kept his eyes to the ground and just kept drinking, refusing to do or say anything of value, to anyone."

Hannah nodded, reasoning that she didn't know Tyler well, but it tracked with his behavior for the night.

"Drake then found Priscilla and derided her and her establishment for a good five minutes, before demanding that she correct his drink order. I mean, I've never seen anyone get so upset about a single cherry!" Seth gestured wildly around the kitchen.

"I see," Hannah said. "And did you happen to note when Drake disappeared?"

Seth stared at her blankly.

"I'm just wondering if we can track when he left the restaurant to get a better idea of who or what was around when he died."

"Nope, no idea. As you can imagine, I had a few other things on my mind. I was trying to clean up after Krystle's temper tantrum so no one else would get hurt." Seth shrugged.

"I understand." She was disappointed at the lack of valuable information Seth had just provided. "Thanks for your time, Seth. I hope things start to turn around for you. And remember, don't be afraid to talk with Ellen about what you said to us."

Seth grunted. "Yeah. Thanks."

Hannah led Colin and Mazie out of the kitchen. "Let's go to the station," she said. "I want to talk with Wendy."

Colin nodded. "Sounds like a good idea to me."

The two of them hopped in Colin's car with Mazie nestled between them in the front seat. When he pulled up, Colin shifted the car into park. "Why don't you head in there? I'll wait in the car with Mazie, but we'll be here if you need us. Just send a text."

"Okay, great. Thank you." Hannah leaned over to kiss her boyfriend's cheek before heading into the station. Once inside, she said hello to Kate and asked if she could be led to Wendy's cell. "I just a have a few questions to ask her. I want to find out who to question next."

Kate and Hannah had a great working relationship, Kate learning to trust Hannah's instincts and investigative skills over their time together. "What does your gut tell you about Wendy?" she asked Hannah.

She shrugged in response. "I can't say for sure yet, it would have been very quick, I was only just speaking to her. Maybe it's because she's a local girl, maybe it's because I feel bad about the way her fiancé was treating her, maybe I think she's innocent, but the only way to know for sure is to ask her a few more questions."

"Sounds good," Kate said, leading her down the hall to Wendy. When they arrived, Wendy was curled up in a ball on the cot in the jail cell. She wasn't crying at that moment, but if the mascara streaks down her face told the story, she'd only recently stopped.

"I'll leave you to it," Kate whispered before walking away.

"Wendy?" Hannah called gently.

Wendy's body stirred and she made a grunting sound.

"Hey, Wendy. My name is Hannah Barry. I'm a local private investigator, and I'm here to ask you a few questions."

Wendy remained motionless.

She tried again. "I don't think you did it, Wendy. Would you talk to me, answer a few questions so that I can find out who did?"

At this, Wendy stretched out her legs. Then she slowly raised herself to a sitting position, her back leaning against the brick wall behind her. Her eyes were cast down at her legs. "What do you want to know?" Her voice was meek, but Hannah thought she detected a hint of hope.

"To begin, how are you feeling?"

Wendy sniffled. "I've been better. I'm trying to remain hopeful, but I know how all of this looks. I was found standing above a dead body, holding a murder weapon. I mean, things simply can't get more unfortunate than that."

Hannah waited. She agreed but felt Wendy may have more to say.

"The thing is, I didn't do it. That's all you have to go off of, my word."

"Are you able to talk to me about anyone who may have had an issue with Drake?"

"To be honest, I didn't know Tyler's family very well. And now I realize that might have been the only reason he and I ever made it as far as we did. What I do know, is that Krystle hated me from the minute we met."

Hannah tilted her head to the side. "Why is that?"

Wendy glowered. "She hated me, because of the fact that Tyler was marrying first. To any normal family, this would be no big deal, but for the Callahan family, it meant that Tyler was one step closer to the first grandchild. And the first grandchild is one step closer to the inheritance."

"What inheritance?" Hannah asked, her curiosity spiked through the roof now.

"Drake had his trust set up so that the first grandchild would get the larger share of the inheritance," Wendy said, her eyes blazing now, meeting Hannah's directly. "I didn't know about it until Tyler casually mentioned it one day after I commented on how much disdain Krystle seemed to have for me. He almost off handedly dropped that fact in."

Hannah felt her heart rate beat in her throat. "This is certainly interesting," Hannah said calmly. "Well, listen. Thank you for your time. I'm going to do my best to get you out of here; in the meantime, try to stay calm and not worry too much."

Wendy looked at Hannah with the saddest eyes she had ever seen. A single tear trickled down her cheek.

"I know, I'm sorry. That's easier said than done, but trust me, I'll be working hard to get you out, and I'll keep you posted."

"Thanks," Wendy whispered before curling back up into a ball.

As Hannah walked back down the hallway to the exit, she passed by Kate's office. The chief of police raised her hand in the air to call Hannah inside. Hannah opened the door to pop her head in. "What is it?" she asked.

"I want to hear what you found out from Wendy, but first, I have something to show you." She handed Hannah a manila envelope. Hannah tipped it so that three crisp white pages slipped out. She examined them. Then turned her gaze to Kate with curiosity. "I'm not an expert in deciphering autopsy reports but does this mean what I think it does?"

Kate smiled. "If you think it means that the blow to Drake's head occurred post-mortem, then yes."

"So, he didn't die from the piece of wood?" Her breath caught.

Kate pointed further down on the page. "No, and in fact, it says that he died from anaphylaxis." Her eyes were ablaze with possibility.

"Whoa," Hannah breathed, her hands beginning to shake. "This opens up a lot of new possibilities."

"Do you know of anything Drake was allergic to, by chance?" Kate asked.

Hannah cast a glance down the hall to where Wendy was in holding. "I have no idea, but you know I'll go find out. Would you go release Wendy now, since we know she is no longer a suspect?"

"Well, we will release her because we have no legal reason to hold her now, but it doesn't mean she's no longer a suspect. Remember how we've talked about keeping our feelings at bay during investigations?"

Hannah nodded. "I remember! But only when you remind me!" Hannah was an excellent investigator because she always followed her gut, but that was the one thing she and Kate disagreed on. Kate followed facts; Hannah followed feelings. "I'll keep it in mind, but for now, she's free, right?"

"Right," Kate confirmed.

Hannah all but raced out to the car where Colin was waiting. Breathless, she opened the door and plopped into the passenger seat. "Did you happen to hear anything about Drake having allergies?" she asked.

Colin let out a chuckle. "And hello to you, too, Hannah." He smiled at his girlfriend.

"Oh, right." She leaned to kiss him on the cheek.

"I didn't hear anything," Colin said. "But it was interesting when he got so angry at the waitress for putting a cherry in his drink. I thought it was because he was rude, but maybe it was because he was worried?"

Hannah's eyes lit up. "That's so true," she said. "I'd forgotten about that. It's a good lead. We don't know his allergies, but I know someone who would."

Colin started the car. "So off to find Tyler, then?"

"Yep," Hannah replied, scooping Mazie onto her lap for some comfort.

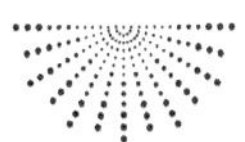

CHAPTER SIX

After driving from Priscilla's Place to every hotel in town, Hannah and Colin sat in the parking lot of a local bar, scratching their heads about what to do next. Hannah had texted all of her contacts and no one had seen Tyler. "How does a guy like Tyler disappear entirely in a place like Blairstown?" Hannah asked. "I would have thought he'd make a splash wherever he went."

"Hmm, it is surprising," Colin agreed. "But he sort of flies under the radar, doesn't he? I think it seems like he makes a splash wherever he goes... because Krystle is with him."

Hannah was thoughtful. "You know, come to think of it, you may be right." She thought back to the party that evening. Though Tyler was in the center of the action for most of the drama, he wasn't the outspoken one. In fact, Hannah specifically recalled Wendy trying desperately to get him to say anything. "So, we redirect our search and try to find Krystle," she said.

"Absolutely," he replied, starting the ignition once more. He gripped his hands on the steering wheel and turned to Hannah. "Um, where do we find Krystle?"

Hannah laughed. "Let's start with their hotel. Then, we can just work back through the series of locations we just did, but this time for Tyler's sister!" She didn't need to verbalize the fact that had they thought about it earlier, they could have been looking for either one of the siblings. The two of them drove in comfortable silence to the hotel the Callahan's were staying in, Hannah petting Mazie's snoozing head as they went.

When they pulled up at the hotel, Hannah and Colin both went inside. They knew which floor Tyler was staying on and assumed the same for Krystle but didn't make it as far as the elevators before they heard her shrill voice echoing from the hotel bar. "No one in the family likes that woman. There's no way the wedding will move forward. She's just not our type of people," Krystle said.

Hannah recognized the vague slur in her words and

knew she'd been very much enjoying cherry champagne since the engagement party. She exchanged a glance with Colin and redirected him to her location.

"Hi!" Hannah said with false enthusiasm. "Krystle, right? We met tonight at the party," Hannah moved next to her at the bar, her elbow resting on it as she started the conversation.

Krystle's glazed eyes scanned the length of Hannah's body. "I don't remember you."

The man Krystle had been speaking with looked relieved at the interruption and backed away from the ladies and rejoined his friends at a nearby table.

"I'm so sorry about what happened to your father tonight," Hannah said.

Krystle's eyes flashed in anger. "So am I. And you can blame *her* for that!" she said.

"Her?" Hannah asked, knowing exactly who Krystle was referring to.

"Yes, Tyler's trailer trash fiancé. She ruined everything!"

Hannah moved closer to Krystle and leaned in conspiratorially. "Do you think she killed your father?"

Krystle frowned and mimicked Hannah's body language. "Of course, she did." Hannah could smell the alcohol on her breath.

"I heard that he died from an allergic reaction, rather than a blow to the head. Do you think Wendy even knew about his allergies?" Hannah asked, knowing Wendy didn't have a clue.

"I'm sure Tyler told her, and she ran with that. She knew we didn't like her, and I bet she wanted us out of the picture. In fact, I feel lucky she didn't find a way to get to me before she was arrested!" Krystle said.

Hannah wasn't sure if it was because Krystle was drunk, or because there were too many holes in her story, but something was definitely off.

"If Wendy did know about the allergies, don't you think it's funny that she was outside of the restaurant when he imbibed his fatal drink?" Hannah asked. Krystle didn't seem to react to the comment. "And if she was the one who gave him the cherry drink, why would she have picked up the bloody stump?" Hannah asked plainly. She didn't think that subtlety was the way forward in Krystle's current state of mind.

Krystle closed her eyes as if to focus on what she'd just said, or shut her out, Hannah couldn't be sure. "Ugh!" she said when she finally opened them again. "Take your suspicions someplace else! Unless you are going to ask me questions about Wendy's guilt, I don't want to hear from you!"

Hannah could see that any value in their conversation was over, so she reluctantly made her way back to Colin and Mazie who were hovering around the entrance to the open bar.

"Did you get any leads?" Colin asked.

She shook her head. "Unfortunately, it wasn't anything concrete, but I have some ideas."

Mazie began jumping, then she seemed to grow increasingly agitated as she spun around, leaping up on her hind legs. Hannah exchanged a glance with Colin. "Is she okay?"

"She was fine until just this moment," he replied. "I have no idea what's gotten into her."

"What I need to do is to get her in a room with the other suspects. I think Mazie can help us."

Colin looked perplexed. "And how do you plan to do that?" he asked.

"Oh!" Hannah said out of the blue. She put her hand up to indicate that he should wait a moment and took out her phone. "Ellen? Hello. I have something to ask you."

CHAPTER SEVEN

The next morning, Ellen knocked on Hannah's office door, bright and early. Hannah was there, waiting for their meeting. The night before she had agreed to talk more about Hannah's idea, but wanted to do it in person.

"All right, tell me what you're thinking," Ellen said with the knowledge that every minute of their time together would be classified as billable.

Hannah got right to it. "I wanted to start by saying that I was able to speak with Seth, and he is in a rough spot."

"Good!" Ellen replied, straightening her shoulders and raising her head.

"I know, there must be a level of satisfaction for you to

hear that news, but we were there to see the disastrous party he threw, and I think he recognized pretty quickly that you are the glue to more than your business relationship. He mentioned that he missed your influence at work, but also in his personal life." Hannah knew this wasn't explicitly part of her job description, but she felt it was important for Ellen to have a full picture of the case.

Ellen crossed her arms and furrowed her brow. "Yeah, well. That's easy to say when you are met with failure. Now he may well recognize that he needs me, but does he actually love me? That's up for debate."

"It's wise of you to be cautious. He also did say that he regrets poaching your clients, for what it's worth."

Ellen shrugged but looked satisfied by that.

Although Hannah thought that Seth might be worthy of a second chance, she sensed that now wasn't the time to press the point with Ellen. Instead, she moved forward with letting Ellen in on her plan for the banquet.

"Thanks for coming today, Ellen. Here is what I wanted to speak with you about. The Callahan family has already planned Drake's funeral and repost. Priscilla will be the hostess."

"What? Priscilla is hosting the banquet at the very restaurant where Drake was poisoned?" Ellen said.

"I know, it's a surprise, but Priscilla insisted on a re-do, even going so far as to offer the event virtually free of charge."

Ellen frowned. "What do you need from me?"

"I was just hoping you would agree to come to the funeral and chat with Seth, maybe get together with both him and Priscilla and work things out. If not for the sake of your marriage, for the sake of your business," Hannah said.

Ellen looked to the ceiling as if to consider the proposal when Hannah was interrupted by the ringing of her cell phone. She stood up and moved away from the couch, mouthing her apologies to Ellen.

"Hello? Oh, hi Kate." Hannah listened intently to the police chief on the other end of the phone.

"Ralph has located Tyler," the police chief said.

"Really? That's amazing news!" Hannah replied.

"It's great news, but here's the shock: Tyler is now claiming responsibility for his father's death. He's saying that he is the one who spiked Drake's usual drink with cherry juice prior to the flute making its way into his father's hands." Hannah sensed that Kate was skeptical about the words she was saying.

"Wow, well, I suppose this is good news then?" Hannah said in the form of a question, as she too was doubting the validity of it.

Ellen had stilled and was watching Hannah intently, waiting for her to report on the conversation.

"So, what's next?" Hannah asked.

"I have to take Tyler into custody. Though I have to say, I'm wondering if the man is simply taking the blame to spare Wendy from further consequences," Kate said.

Hannah wasn't sure about that. "Hm, that doesn't seem to be something Tyler would do. He was so passive about defending her to his family. Do you really think he'd sacrifice his own future?"

"I guess that's a good point," Kate said.

"Not to mention the fact that Wendy is all but free of the charges at this point," Hannah added.

"Fair point. These are excellent considerations, Hannah. I guess I'm just trying to put my finger on something that feels... off," Kate said.

"Do you want me to come to talk to him? Maybe see if I can find out any more information? He might be more willing to talk to someone who isn't police?" Hannah asked.

"Ha! You've read my mind. Get down to the station when you can, I'd love your opinion on his state of mind." She hung up the phone, leaving Hannah to look at Ellen.

"We are agreed, then?" Hannah said. "You'll come to the repast and chat with Seth and Priscilla, hopefully, try to put some of this behind you all?"

Ellen nodded. "I'll do that. But can you tell me what that phone call was about? Did I hear you say Wendy was off the hook now?"

"Yes, once we established the cause of death, Kate had no legal grounds to keep Wendy. Though she's not yet absolved of suspicion."

Ellen nodded thoughtfully. "I see. Well, I wouldn't want to keep you from the rest of this case. Thanks for calling me over here. I think you have the right idea, making Seth and I face one another like adults. There has been so much childish back and forth between us as we navigate this divorce."

Hannah was impressed by Ellen's change of tune. "I agree. I'm glad you feel that way. I'll see you this afternoon then. For now, though, if you'll excuse me, I'm heading to the station to ask Tyler a few questions. I guess he's confessed to killing his father."

Ellen's eyes sparked. "He has?"

"Right?" Hannah said. "I don't believe him either, but I'll go get to the bottom of it."

Ellen left while Hannah hopped in her car to head to the police station. When she arrived, Kate ushered her back to speak directly with Tyler, who was sitting upright in an interrogation room, hands folded on the desk in front of him, looking straight ahead.

"Hi, Tyler," Hannah began.

He sat unmoving.

"I just wanted to speak with you about your recent confession."

His eyes darted towards her for a split second, then settled back on the wall in front of him.

Hannah was beginning to feel desperate. She'd never come across a witness quite as stubborn as this one. "Tyler, I won't make you speak to me. I can't make you speak to me. But I do just want to leave you with the idea that I don't think you're guilty. I think you're here for some other reason, one which I'm not exactly sure of, but I'm looking into it. If there's anything you want to say to me to point me in the right direction, I'm all ears."

Tyler was mute in response.

"Okay." Hannah stood up from the chair opposite Tyler. "I'm heading to your father's repast now. I'll be keeping an ear to the ground."

Tyler's back was stick straight. Hannah couldn't help but be impressed with his commitment to silence. She cast a glance back to him before leaving the room and hopping back in her car to Priscilla's Place. She arrived at the after-funeral banquet just as most others were filing into the restaurant. On the ride over, Hannah sifted through the potential suspects in her mind. Out of everyone, her mind kept catching on to Krystle. She determined to pay special attention to Tyler's sister that afternoon.

When she entered the establishment, she hadn't taken more than three steps in when a pale, blonde girl with steel-blue eyes approached her. The woman gripped Hannah's upper arm with surprising strength and brought her to the side of the room. Hannah allowed it, assuming that their conversation would amount to something useful. It was when they were next to a window, face to face, that Hannah recognized the woman. It was Jessica Klein, one of Priscilla's waitresses. More specifically, the one Drake had scolded about his drink.

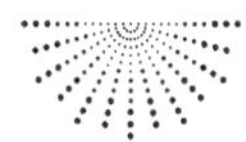

CHAPTER EIGHT

"Jessica!" Hannah said. "I'm sorry I didn't recognize you right away. Is everything okay?"

Jessica looked even more pale than usual; her blue eyes focused hard on Hannah. "I have to tell you something," she said. "I've been feeling guilty since it happened. I'm just... I don't know how to say it." She looked pained and Hannah wanted to comfort her. She rubbed Jessica's arm and said in a soothing voice, "It's okay. Whatever you need to say, you can tell me."

Jessica gulped and nodded solemnly. "Okay. I was the one who served Drake his final drink." She stared at Hannah as if waiting for the blowback. However, Hannah was confused.

"Jessica, I know. That wasn't a crime, you were just doing your job."

"I know, that's what I keep trying to tell myself as well, but obtrusive thoughts keep rearing up. I swear I was careful with the beverage. Priscilla specifically asked me to check the drink before setting it back on my tray. I knew Drake had allergies, I was reminded of them, and yet somehow he still died by my hand!" The poor woman looked like she could keel over right then.

Her story rang little alarm bells in Hannah's mind. "Wait, can you replay exactly what happened to me, one more time?" she asked.

Jessica gulped once and nodded. "Sure. So, Priscilla asked me to check the drink before serving it to Drake. We were all prepped about guests' allergies, so she wanted to be sure Drake didn't get anything with cherry in it. Then Priscilla herself checked the drink and approved it. I was so paranoid about the whole thing that I even conferred with another waitress before serving Drake the drink. I just cannot believe this happened on my watch, Worse than that, by my hand!"

Hannah's mind was now on red alert. The fact that Priscilla herself insisted on checking the drink before it was served, and then that same drink actually killed a man, well, you didn't need to be a private investigator to smell the suspicion in that cherry drink. Then Hannah thought of something else from the night in question. Mazie had been agitated by something in the shadows when she came across the body. Now Hannah was wondering what, or who that could have been.

As she watched the stressed young woman, she knew she needed to comfort her somehow. She placed her hand on Jessica's back. "It's going to be okay. Trust me. I can't explain right now, but I need you to hear that it's not your fault. What happened had nothing to do with you." Hannah was certain of her words, just not quite certain of how to prove them just yet, but her experience told her that would come if she let it. "If you'll excuse me, I need to go get to the bottom of this," she said.

Hannah moved through the crowd towards the puppy play pen. She whispered to Mazie before dropping her in, "Have fun. I'll be back for you; I just need you here for a few moments." She kissed Mazie's snout before turning to join the mourner's meal.

Hannah noticed that Krystle wore her stern, judgmental face as she sat at the head of the table. She found it interesting that Krystle hadn't shown any crack in her veneer, even to reveal any real sadness at her father's death.

Then Hannah's eye saw Priscilla moving swiftly between the kitchen and the guests. She made a beeline towards the woman. "Priscilla, could I speak with you for a moment?" she called after her.

Priscilla stopped and turned at the sound of Hannah's voice. "Oh, hi! Of course. Do you have news about Ellen for me?"

"No, not yet. She's coming by a little bit later. But before she gets here, I wanted to ask you a few questions."

"Oh? Please do. Things are actually going smoothly. I mean, as smoothly as they can be for a post-funeral gathering, but you know," Priscilla shrugged.

Hannah decided to cut through Pricilla's false piety fast and clean. "Just really quickly, what did you do to Drake's drink order the night he died?" she asked simply.

Priscilla didn't show any reaction, Hannah wondered if it was because the tone of her voice was casual, not at all matching with the content of her words. Hannah tried again. "Did you poison Drake?"

That got Priscilla's attention. She tensed and her face grew angry and cold. "How dare you come in here and suggest such a thing. At the man's funeral, no less!"

Hannah appreciated Priscilla's sincerity, and she almost believed her. "Jessica mentioned that you triple checked the man's drink. You were the last point of contact before it was served to him. How else should we interpret that?"

Priscilla opened her mouth in reply when Hannah pressed on. "Not to mention the fact that my dog, Mazie, saw something lurking in the shadows of the scene of the crime. Could it have been you? Were you in the alleyway, lurking, trying to make sure that your poison had done its job?"

Something akin to panic flashed across Priscilla's face. Hannah was convinced she had her until Priscilla spoke. "Drake did in fact threaten me," she said in a low voice. "He said he'd blacken the restaurant's name if the event didn't run smoothly." Her eyes were wide and scared.

Hannah couldn't help but smirk. "So, it was you. You were trying to ensure that Drake didn't ruin your place of business."

Priscilla shook her head vigorously. "No, that's not it at all." She glanced frantically around the room until her eyes fell on the puppy playpen. "Watch this. Follow me." The woman rushed across the room away from Hannah. For a moment Hannah thought she was making a run for it when she saw her stop at the playpen. She crouched down to make eye contact with Mazie, and Hannah held her breath. Mazie's reaction would tell if she was the murderer.

Waiting for her beagle to snarl in response, Hannah was surprised when Mazie simply jumped up on her hind legs and wagged her tail at Priscilla. The woman laughed in response, pressing her cheek against the bars of the playpen so the dog could lick her face. By now Hannah had made her way over. "Priscilla, I believe I owe you an apology. I can't explain how you aren't guilty, but you obviously aren't or Mazie would not be reacting to you like this."

Still kneeling, Priscilla looked up at Hannah, gratitude flooded her eyes. "She'd smell me, or she'd recognize me. I know how smart these dogs are. I'm just grateful she was here because I can't express to you just how much I was not involved in that murder," she said.

Hannah held her hand out to the woman to help her to stand. "I'm sorry I blamed you. I trust Mazie on this one." She tentatively touched Priscilla's arm. "My dog wouldn't have been so trusting of you had you been guilty, and I trust her." She wrapped Priscilla in a big hug, and the woman sagged in relief in her arms.

Then Ellen appeared at the door of the restaurant. When she saw the two women, a large smile brightened her face. "Ladies! Just the two people I came looking for."

Hannah pulled away from Priscilla to give Ellen a greeting hug, as the woman skipped towards them. As she came closer, Hannah heard a low growl behind her. It started quietly at a level Hannah may not even have heard, but then it grew louder and louder. When Ellen came to embrace Hannah, Mazie began barking loudly.

Mazie was barking frantically, jumping up and down to the extent that even Hannah couldn't calm her down. Colin's head turned at the ruckus and came running over. He crouched down and tried calling her name in a soothing voice, but the beagle didn't seem to hear him. Next, he stepped into the puppy playpen, sitting next to Mazie, but she just kept jumping up and down. Now her paws were on the gate as she growled, looking out of it.

Hannah watched her dog carefully and though she wasn't entirely sure, she had her suspicions. She gave her dog a reassuring pat on the head. "Thanks, Mazie. I'll take it from here." Then she slipped her a small treat and gestured for Colin to join her in the eating area. The two of them walked arm in arm into the room. Hannah immediately noticed Krystle's demeanor. She seemed to be positively glowing. Hannah walked over to her.

"You seem to be holding up okay," Hannah said.

Krystle turned to her. "Of course, I'm okay. That silly woman who tried to trick my brother out of his inheritance is neutralized, and Tyler himself is behind bars. I'm always happy when justice is being served." She smiled, tilting her glass to Hannah.

Hannah felt her adrenaline rush to her ears. This woman was so smug, and at her own father's funeral. The nerve. Colin watched Hannah's reaction and knowingly leaned down to whisper in her ear. "Are you about to deal her the final blow?"

Hannah shook her head and turned to speak in a hushed tone. "She's still a likely suspect, and a terrible person, but she's not the murderer. "Wait here," she whispered. She went out to the puppy playpen and clipped Mazie's leash onto her. Then they slowly made their way back to the spot in the room where Ellen was holding court. As she approached, Hannah heard her telling the other guests how *she* was happy to plan all of their upcoming affairs, in an even finer establishment than the one they were currently sitting in. Hannah gritted her teeth and thought about the divorce settlement coming her way. That must be how she secured a nice, new event space.

Then Hannah saw Seth awkwardly ambling towards Ellen, and she thought he must be ready to make peace. She was grateful Ellen came today for him to have the opportunity to do so. Seth stopped in front of his ex-wife and stood in a submissive position with his head bowed and his hands clasped in front of him. "Thanks for coming here today," he said, peering at her through his eyelashes.

She stood, waiting.

"I just wanted to say how much I've missed you."

She grunted.

Now Seth's voice shook with nerves. "And how regretful I am to have poached Priscilla as a client. That was the wrong thing to do, and it made me realize how grateful I am for your love and support all of these years." He looked at her to see her arms crossed and a single hip jutting out. "Would you consider forgiving me? T-taking me back?" he asked timidly.

Ellen smiled a warm, loving smile. "Oh, Seth," she began, causing his eyes to meet hers with hope.

At that moment Priscilla also walked up to the couple. "Ellen, thank you for coming here tonight. I'm so grateful you are willing to hear us out," she said.

Ellen's gaze then shifted to something more sinister when she leveled her eyes at the two of them standing before her. "Seth, it will be cold day in hell when I take you back. What you did isn't just washed away with an apology. Now I'll spend my days poaching back *your* clients. And as for you, Priscilla, I'll be taking great pleasure in steering potential customers away from the space where a man was murdered. Can you imagine? A client researching venues and planners online, only to find out that one or both was associated with a death? At an event?"

Priscilla's face fell. Seth shrunk down even further. Meanwhile, Ellen seemed to be taking great pleasure in all of it as she glared at them both. "I don't know. If it were me, it would put me off." Her cold eyes startled even Hannah. She never had any intention of coming here to reconcile or even to hear Seth out. She just wanted to humiliate him. Hannah shook her head at her own naivety.

Then Mazie bounded forward, the leash pulling away from Hannah's hand. She was growling as she launched herself at Ellen's purse and began sniffing through it, rifling through all of the items with her nose. By now the entire room had stilled to better hear Ellen's monologue and an audible series of gasps filled the previously quiet space. Mazie scratched and sniffed so hard that Ellen's entire bag was turned inside out. Gum, lipstick, her wallet, and slips of paper were strewn about when another circular container fell out. In clear, bold words running along the side, it said *makeup putty*.

Hannah watched as Ellen's eyes flashed wide and she scrambled to pick the item up. Hannah thought it was odd to be so protective over a tube of makeup when a memory hit her like a flash. At their original meeting, the one where Ellen was so insistent that Hannah take the case, she suggested Hannah going to the party dressed in costume, or a disguise. She studied Ellen's face with a new curiosity, taking in all of her features in minute detail. She quietly walked up beside Priscilla and whispered something in her ear, gesturing to Ellen. Then she went to find Jessica and asked her the same thing. "Take a long, hard look at Ellen. Is there anything familiar about the woman?"

Jessica was taken aback and confused but did as she was asked. Something like realization seemed to flicker across her face when Hannah continued. "You mentioned that you conferred with one more waitress after Priscilla double-checked your drink. Is that right?"

Jessica nodded.

"Is there a chance that person could have been the waitress? Does she look at all familiar?"

On the other side of her, Priscilla gasped. She saw it first, likely because she knew Ellen both with and without the disguise. "It was her!" she whispered to Hannah. "It was Ellen who was dressed up as the waitress! I remember thinking that the woman was heavily made-up but chalked it up to her covering up from a hard night. Admittedly, I was very distracted at the event so wasn't taking into account many details, but now I see it clearly. It was actually Ellen!"

Jessica stared harder at the woman and nodded slowly. "I think you are right. I'd recognize those eyes anywhere. They flashed between kind and sinister the whole night; I remember feeling on uneven footing as far as where I stood with her. She was pretty up and down all night, but I, too, was stressed myself so wasn't paying close attention."

Krystle, who'd been standing close by, suddenly spoke up. "If you three are talking about Ellen over there, I had consulted with her before hiring Seth to take charge of the party. We spoke enough that we got to the point of me explaining about Drake's allergies. I wanted to be sure the party planner knew how important it was to accommodate for it. Turns out she knew how to accommodate for it, just in a different way."

Hannah had heard enough. She marched over to Ellen and squared her shoulders to the woman. "Was this your plan all along? You kill Drake by slipping him cherries, knowing he's allergic to them. Then, you make sure that everyone hears about what a failure Seth's party is, and how awful Priscilla's restaurant is?" Hannah's eyes were flaring with anger, but Ellen seemed unphased.

"Really," she said.

"Whatever happened to you telling me that everything works out as it should? This seems a little manipulative for that sort of attitude." Hannah's voice was raising now, and the whole room was listening.

Ellen, never at a loss for words, tensed. Meanwhile, Priscilla stood up an inch straighter, and Seth's confidence seemed bolstered enough to confront his ex. He walked up to the woman, no longer showing contrition. "So maybe I couldn't make our marriage work, but did you have to go to *such* extremes?" he asked. He ran a hand through his hair, now looking pained. "I mean, murder? Really, Ellen? Even for you, that's a level beyond!"

Ellen put her hands out. "Seth, Priscilla, it's not what it seems. I promise you. Please, give me a chance to explain."

But it was difficult to hear any more of what she wanted to say, as Mazie's barking began reaching a frantic pitch. The dog began circling Ellen, jumping and baring her teeth at the woman. Hannah hadn't seen Mazie react like that to anyone, and she knew her suspicions had been confirmed.

"Mazie! Come here, girl. It's okay!" she called out over the crowd. Mazie lowered her growl to a low rumble and kept her eyes on Ellen as she reversed her way back to Hannah. The former police dog sat next to Hannah on high alert, her eyes continuously trained on Ellen.

When there was a level of calm, Hannah spoke out over the crowd. "My trusty beagle here is to be credited for solving much of this crime. She has such a strong sense of character and intent that I knew Wendy wasn't guilty on the night of the murder because Mazie went out of her way to comfort the poor woman following Drake's death. For that reason, I made it my mission to find the true killer. Now, tonight, Mazie has confirmed my suspicions. She's made it very clear to all of us that Ellen is our prime suspect. She recognizes the woman from dressing up as a waitress; in fact, the very waitress who spiked Drake's drink. Ladies and gentlemen," Hannah said, addressing the crowd and loving the attention, "Ellen may not be in a costume any longer, but she is no less guilty!" Her pronouncement rang out through the room and collectively, the crowd took a step away from the guilty woman.

Ellen's face grew pale and sweat beaded on her brow. Her eyes glazed over even as she surveyed the room. She gripped at her throat before spontaneously reaching for a cake knife next to her, and before anyone could see it coming, she was charging towards Hannah.

Hannah's instincts seemed to be on a delay, but the same couldn't be said for both Mazie and Colin. They each leaped to action; Mazie running to bite the calf of the charging woman and Colin leaning down, angling his shoulder to Ellen's stomach to take her down in a football tackle. Their decisive actions stopped Hannah from enduring any real harm, but after the shock of the moment wore off, Hannah surveyed her boyfriend on the floor, pinning Ellen beneath him with his arms and his knees, while Mazie stayed gripped on the woman's calf. Jessica was quick to follow and assist Colin with holding her down. Meanwhile, Ellen called out in pain, "Get off of me! Get them off of me!"

Hannah scoffed as she reached for her phone. "Right. They'll get off of you just as soon as the police arrive," she said. As she dialed Kate's number, Hannah noticed that in the chaos, she hadn't come out unscathed. She had endured a slash to her forearm, the blood was a deep red and she could see that the cut ran deep. "Colin," she croaked. She kept her composure as she stared at her boyfriend.

"I've got it from here," Jessica said, relieving Colin of the pressure to restrain Ellen. Then Kate's voice echoed through Hannah's phone. Colin picked it up and explained where they were and what had happened. "Don't forget to send an ambulance as well!" he said into the receiver. While they waited for official backup, Colin applied pressure to Hannah's wound. She slumped back to lean against the wall and slid down to a sitting position.

"I'm fine, Colin. Don't worry about me," she said, though her voice was lighted and lilting.

Just as she heard the sirens approach in the distance, she felt herself grow a little bit woozy. "Stay with me, Hannah!" Colin said, just as she fainted into his arms.

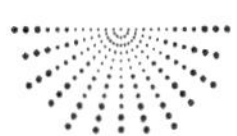

CHAPTER TEN

Hannah woke to the sound of a steady beeping interrupting her peaceful dream of laying on a beach in Hawaii. The sun was replaced by angry, blinking florescent lights and she felt something itching her nose. She reached a hand up to feel the tube stuffed up inside of it. She blinked twice, trying to get her bearings, then turned to see Colin staring at her, concern across his face. She smiled through her haze, and he smiled back. Taking her hand he squeezed gently. Then he lifted Mazie up so her tricolored head was visible at the bedside. Mazie frantically tried to climb on the bed, her front paws inching closer to Hannah as she licked her owner's cheek lovingly.

Hannah laughed, realizing now that she was in a hospital. "How did you manage to sneak Mazie in here?" she asked, delighted that he had figured it out.

"Ah, you might remember that Mazie still has her credentials as a police dog. She's totally legitimate, I didn't even have to sneak her!" he said, delighted, but not as delighted as Hannah. She reached over to embrace her loyal companion and buried her face in Mazie's neck. "You're the best," she said, her voice muffled. "How long have I been passed out?" Hannah asked, looking around the room, still slightly dazed from sleep.

"Not too long, but so much has happened since you got to the hospital," Colin replied.

This perked Hannah's ears up, and she elbowed her way to sitting. "Tell me everything," she said, slightly more alert. Mazie, meanwhile, nuzzled closer to her owner.

"Kate did some asking around, and Ellen has been identified by other members of Priscilla's waitstaff as well. Not only that, but the lab results are already back, and it turns out that her fingerprints are all over the fatal glass that Drake drank from." Colin wagged his eyebrows waiting for the meaning to set in for Hannah.

"So, they have proof?" she asked.

"Indeed, they do," he replied.

Hannah lay back down on her pillow and stared at the ceiling for a few moments. "I can't believe Ellen used me so blatantly to help her own case," she said.

"How do you mean?" Colin asked.

"Well, she obviously set Seth and Priscilla up, she knew she would kill Drake at their event to essentially put them out of business, driving all of her poached clients and any Seth had on his own list, right to her books." Hannah took a breath as if the speaking labored her.

Colin placed a hand on her shoulder, and she felt the comfort of it enough to go on. "She had no regard for Wendy and Tyler's fates, happy to let them waste away in jail. Not to mention Drake's actual life she stole from him. It was everyone else be damned," Hannah said. "And she brought me into it knowing that Seth poached her clients, and not needing me to solve any crime at all. She just wanted me on her side, so I'd have evidence against her ex-husband, making him look guilty of the crime." Hannah shook her head in disgust. "What a terrible person Ellen is. And the worst thing is that I had no idea. I thought she was great. I'm worried my sixth sense might be fading." She looked at Colin, concerned.

He moved his hand through her hair and kissed her forehead. "People like Ellen are excellent at tricking others. She had us all fooled, that's nothing for you to feel bad about," he said. "As far as your sixth sense goes, you knew exactly who killed Drake before all of us did. You knew in your gut, you just needed to find the evidence to prove it, so that's very definitely intact."

Hannah's eyes softened as she listened to him reassure her, hoping he'd continue. He tucked a strand of hair behind her ears and looked on lovingly. "As far as her using you to get people on her side, well, you got paid for your time, and I think we can all agree she chose the wrong investigator to trick, because you did end up solving the murder, and she has the pleasure of paying for your services." His eyes danced with mischief and Hannah couldn't help but laugh.

"You make a great point. Ellen just paid for me to investigate her into jail," she said. "But I couldn't have done it without this little one," she said, kissing Mazie on top of her head. The little beagle released a little sigh and lifted her chin onto Hannah's arm. She smiled then looked at Colin. "Or you," she said. Then she gingerly lifted her arm all wrapped in white gauze. "And I only had to suffer a minor injury in the line of fire."

Colin held the exposed fingers peeking out from under the gauze. "Tyler was officially released from jail, and he and Wendy were quick to reconcile when he got out."

Hannah's eyebrows lifted. "Really? That surprises me. I didn't think their relationship was going to be reparable after their fight with Krystle."

"No kidding. I thought the same thing, but you know what they say about tragedy bringing people closer together. Maybe they were able to remember what was most important to them when they had all of that alone time in the cells," Colin said.

"Maybe so. So, they're fully back together, engaged and everything?" Hannah asked.

"The ring is back on her finger and the whole thing!" Colin confirmed.

"Well, I guess that's kind of romantic," Hannah replied, her eyes closing. She felt herself slipping back into sleep, unable to fight her eyelids awake.

"They gave you lots of meds, Hannah. Just let sleep take you. It'll do you wonders to have all of that rest."

Hannah heard his voice in what sounded like a tiny chamber as she slipped further and further down into sleep. She felt Colin's hand on her face and managed to turn to kiss the palm of his hand, she tried to tell him that she looked forward to going home with him but couldn't be sure if she said it out loud, or if it stayed in her head.

Just before she lost herself to sleep once more, she heard Colin's faint whisper in her ear, "We have so much to discuss once you are back to full strength."

CHAPTER ELEVEN

The following week, the same group of people found themselves back at Priscilla's Place yet again. This time they were there enjoying yet another engagement party for Wendy and Tyler, though the mood of this gathering was decidedly more festive. Music played loudly, people danced with abandon on the dance floor, drinks were flowing, and there wasn't a cherry in sight. Wendy and Tyler stood holding hands while beaming at their guests, both flush with joy and love.

A recovered Hannah hooked her own arm into Colin's as they enjoyed a dance together. Colin swung her expertly, turning her and dipping her as if they were professional ballroom dancers. Though he was careful not to put too much pressure on her injured arm, the two of them had a ball celebrating.

As they floated around the room, Hannah overheard Krystle speaking to a friend of hers. "I'm not entirely sure about Wendy still. The union certainly wouldn't be one of my choosing," she said. Hannah slowed down so she could hear the rest, pulling Colin's arm back to her. "In the end, though, I have to hand it to both Wendy and Tyler, they offered to split my dad's inheritance equally between us, rather than take the bulk of it once they have a child." The person Krystle spoke to nodded with disinterest and took her leave, providing a perfect opportunity for Hannah to step in.

"Hi, Krystle!" she said. "That's wonderful news about the inheritance. What made Tyler decide to do that?"

Krystle looked slightly startled, then shrugged nonchalantly as if she didn't care who she was speaking with, just as long as she had an audience. "I'm not sure what exactly made them change their minds, but I'm sure time in jail has a way of recalibrating one's priorities," she said.

Hannah privately thought that it might do Krystle some good to spend time alone, processing her own life, but she kept that to herself. Out loud, she said, "Do you think Wendy might have had something to do with it?" She knew Wendy from around town but had really gotten to know her better throughout the investigation. Her instincts that she was a smart, kind girl turned out to be very true, and she had her suspicions that Wendy was the one who convinced Tyler to split the inheritance with his sister.

Krystle paused. "You know, I hadn't thought about it. If so, I already like her more!"

Hannah suppressed a smile. That was too easy. "If you don't mind my asking, why did your father have such a strange inheritance policy with his estate?"

Krystle gave her signature shrug, although Hannah was beginning to realize the shrug was less about not caring than it was about covering up her real feelings. "That's a great question. Our father was an excellent business-man, that can't be argued, but it was almost as if he brought his competitive nature home and pit my brother and me against one another in order to promote the fighting spirit."

Hannah thought about that for a moment, wondering how any pair of siblings could get along with a relation-ship like that. "How do you think that worked out for you both?" she asked.

"Well, needless to say, we fight all of the time. But under it all there is a big love between us. I only want what's best for him. Wendy isn't like anyone he's dated before, or anyone our family has ever interacted with, to be honest, so she gave me a pause, but to be truthful, she's growing on me." Krystle cast a quick glance in Wendy's direction. "Also, it's a bit of nature versus nurture, as they say. I think we can all agree that I was born with more of a fighting spirit, much like my father, while Tyler is a little more passive." She smiled as she watched her brother.

"It sounds to me as if you two are going to work things out and develop a new kind of relationship without your father there pitting you against one another," Hannah said.

"God rest his soul," Krystle replied. "But yes. I think you are onto something."

"Well, cheers to you, then!" Hannah said, grabbing a glass of champagne from a passing server and clinked Krystle's glass.

Then Priscilla emerged from behind a set of velvet drapes looking positively cheerful. Just looking at her joy brought a smile to Hannah's face. Priscilla moved through the crowd in search of someone, and when she found that person, she shared a quick kiss with him. Absently, Hannah considered that she didn't even know Priscilla was dating anyone. Then the man turned around and Hannah's hand reached out to grab Colin's upper arm instinctively. Colin turned to follow Hannah's gaze and released a little chuckle. "Well, there you go. Will wonders never cease," he said. Hannah couldn't tear her eyes away from the new couple. "Seth and Priscilla. I never would have predicted it, but when it's staring back at you like that, it kind of makes sense, doesn't it?" she said not tearing her eyes away from the two of them.

"They do seem like a great match," Colin agreed. After a few more songs on the dance floor, Colin and Hannah stepped off, breathing heavily from the exertion.

"I can't remember the last time I had this much fun!" Hannah said.

"This is a blast," Colin agreed. "What do you think, should we take a little break and go check on Mazie?"

As soon as they'd stepped into Priscilla's Place, Mazie made a beeline straight for the puppy playpen. She loved it in there with her friends and the treats Priscilla provided. Hannah had to hand it to the woman, she knew how to throw a party that made everyone happy.

When the two of them made their way to the playpen, Hannah reached down to clip a leash on Mazie's harness. "Should we go for a walk, girl?" she asked her dog, who replied with giant tail wags back and forth.

"Looks like a yes to me," Colin said, smiling. The trio walked out into the evening air and Colin breathed in deeply. "Do you just feel it?" he asked.

"Feel what?" Hannah said.

"That love is in the air?"

Hannah nodded. "I really do. Watching Wendy and Tyler tonight, they seemed to be in their groove, now that their family dynamics have been resolved, it seemed as if they were a couple that is meant to be," she replied.

"I can think of another couple as well," Colin said with a twinkle in his eye.

Hannah smiled at him. "Oh, of course! Seth and Priscilla, there is nothing like new love, am I right?" she replied. Hannah knew who Colin was really referring to but thoroughly enjoyed teasing him along the way.

"Yes, Priscilla and Seth are so cute. And there is just one more couple I was thinking about."

Hannah looked deeply into Colin's eyes and smiled. "Hmm, who could I be missing, I wonder?"

Colin stopped and grabbed both of her hands in his. He brought her closer to him and gave her a shy smile. "I'm thinking about us," he said.

Hannah grinned. "I know. I'm thinking about us, too." She tilted her chin up for a kiss. She wasn't sure the direction this conversation was headed in, but she did know enough not to get her hopes up for a proposal. There were many opportunities she thought Colin could have taken to pop the question, so she just had to settle into the fact that it may not happen any time soon. Most recently, he could have asked for her hand in marriage when she woke up in the hospital, but when he hadn't done so, she realized she had misjudged the timing yet again.

Just as Colin moved his lips to meet hers, Mazie zoomed around and bumped into his leg. "Ouch!" he cried, dropping down to hold his shin. "What was that about, Mazie?" he asked the dog.

Hannah looked around looking for the cause of Mazie's outburst. Was there another showdown lurking around?

Then she noticed Colin reaching into his pocket while he was still on his knees. He met her eyes and brought one leg up to balance on his foot while leaving the other leg bent. Hannah's eyes flew open in surprise. "Whoa, wait – what?" She couldn't believe what she was seeing.

A slow and steady smile crept across Colin's face as he removed his hand from his pocket and presented a small, velvet, blue box. Hannah pressed both palms to her mouth as Colin flipped the lid of the box open to reveal a beautiful, sparkling trio of diamonds. The center stone was a princess cut, glistening every which way under the moonlight, and cast on either side of it were small yellow trillion cut diamonds. "Hannah Barry, would you do me the honor of marrying me?" he asked. The simple statement held so much meaning between them. Hannah was worried if she spoke, every word she'd ever known would come pouring out of her. Instead, she released an uncontrolled squeal and nodded her head in a vigorous *yes*. Then she dropped down on both of her own knees and held Colin's face in her hands. "I can't believe this is actually happening!" she said. "I've been waiting so long for this moment!"

Colin smiled. "So have I. I've been wanting to pop the question for so long, and have almost done it so many times before, but I just wanted everything to be so perfect that the moment never felt right. I realized when I saw you in the hospital bed, hurt, that I had to do it. I couldn't waste any more time."

"I'm so glad you did," she replied.

He looked up to the sky and pointed at the moon. "I wanted moonlight to make the moment perfect," he said.

Hannah followed his gaze. "This moment feels pretty perfect to me," she replied. Colin took her face in his hands, and they shared a tender kiss to mark the beginning of their forever, together. Then he took her ring finger with her new ring on it and held it for her to examine. "I chose three stones, one for you, one for me, and one for Mazie," he said, scratching the dog behind her ears until her hind leg was shaking back and forth with delight.

"That's the sweetest thing I've ever heard," Hannah said. "Almost as sweet as you are." She leaned in for one more kiss from her new fiancé, while Mazie yapped happily, spinning around the happy pair.

IF YOU MISSED any of these fabulous fun cozy mysteries grab the first 6 here or read on for a preview of this great value box set.

Hannah looked up at the vibrant colors on the trees lining her street. The cheerful red and rich auburn of the leaves were in direct contrast to her mood. *How can the leaves be so happy when they are about to fall to their death?* She was just one block from her cozy little house where she'd curl up by the fire, drink some cider, and feel sorry for herself. She just had to make it past his house first. It was enough that she lived one block from Peter Royce, her ex-boyfriend. But now she had to pass by his home every single day on her morning walk. She wrapped her scarf up over her nose and tucked her head down into it. Maybe he wouldn't see her.

It was then that she heard the squeal of tires and watched as a little blue sports car took a tight, tidy turn into Peter's driveway. She felt her blood run cold and her feet involuntarily stopped moving. Out of the driver's seat popped a stylish, petite brunette wearing a shade of bright pink lipstick. The foolish man had always preferred brunette's, saying her blonde was a little washed out.

The new woman slipped gracefully up the front steps of the house and there, waiting for her, was Peter. His tall frame filled the doorway, he wrapped the brunette into a tight squeeze and gave her a kiss on the lips. Hannah knew he hadn't been faithful; that's why they'd broken up. But she didn't think she'd have to watch him with his new girlfriend with her very own eyes. She felt acid rise in her throat and hid behind a big oak tree, taking deep breaths in and out. When she heard his front door close, she looked up to the crisp, blue sky.

Oh, you've got a lot of nerve looking bright and beautiful on a day like today. Can't you see that people down here are suffering? If she couldn't yell at Peter, she'd yell at the sky.

Slamming her hand in her pocket she pulled out her phone. Maybe checking on her precious few house listings would distract her. "Ugh, no alerts!" she muttered and toggled over to her bank app to see what her current balance was. More depression and a big gulp. "I guess I'll have to dip into my savings again this month." Pressing her fingers into the tender skin under her eyes she bit down. "I will not cry today. I will not cry today." However, she did need to sell a house. And soon.

When she arrived at her own cozy little place a smile came to her lips. Colorful potted plants lining the front porch and filling her with joy, she felt her shoulders relax. It was time for that cider. But when she walked up the steps to her door, she was startled by a deep voice.

"Hey cuz! Did you forget we were meeting today?"

Hannah jumped as if an armed thug had just accosted her, throwing her hand to her heart to steady the erratic beating. "Ahhh!" she shrieked, momentarily startled out of her self-pity. Then the familiar curly blond hair of her cousin finally registered. "Niles! Oh, I'm so sorry. I did completely space out our meeting today. But it's so nice to see a familiar face." She let herself sink into the empty spot beside him on the porch swing.

Niles' long legs stretched to the railing. His easy grin turned up at the corners of his mouth. "Well, did you at least remember that I was bringing a surprise for you?"

Hannah lifted her brows in anticipation. "My favorite donuts? This is the perfect day for some of those."

Niles shook his head.

"A macchiato? That would also be a lovely treat."

His grin got wider, but he shook his head again.

"Fine, I give up." She crossed her legs under her body and turned to face Niles.

"I know you've been going through a tough time lately. And I really want to help make you feel better about things."

Despite herself, Hannah felt the well of tears forming. Swallowing, she strained her eyes and willed them not to fall.

"I wish I could be here more to help out, but as I can't... I've arranged for a proxy."

Hannah looked into Niles' deep blue eyes, searching for something to help her understand.

He stood up, stretching to his full height, his head ducking his six-foot frame to avoid a hanging plant. "Close your eyes."

Hannah obediently placed her hands over her face. "This better be good."

She heard the shuffle of Niles' feet across the wood beams of her porch move away from her, and then come back. Then she felt the warm, wet slide of something move up her cheek. "What in the world?" she lurched back in her seat, dropping her hands from her face.

OMG, sitting proudly on the porch swing and staring at her with big, brown eyes shining playfully, was a... dog. It looked at Hannah. Waiting.

Hannah released a nervous chuckle and turned to Niles. "Heh, heh. Good one! Is this your way of cheering me up, by joking about getting me a puppy?" She placed her hands on her lap and gave the dog a sideways glance. It was still staring at her.

"Actually," Niles said. "She's not a puppy. She's three years old, and her name is Mazie.

Hannah looked at the tricolored dog with floppy ears and a long tail. "So, is it a bulldog?"

Niles laughed. "Not a dog person, are you? This is a beagle. They are some of the most loyal, lovable, and intelligent dogs you will ever come across. And this little sweetie is also one of the bravest dogs you'll ever know. She was shot in the line of duty and saved someone's life in the process." Niles scratched behind Mazie's ears, causing her tail to flop cheerfully against the cushion.

An unconscious smile began to form on one side of Hannah's mouth. "Cute. Mazie, you're a cutie." Then she looked at Niles. "Well, it worked, she cheered me up. Thanks for the surprise. Should we head inside to warm up?" She lifted herself from the swing.

"Well, that was easier than I thought it would be. So, you'll take her?" Niles asked.

Hannah spun around to face him. "*Take her?* What do you mean, I thought you just brought her by for a visit?"

Niles' face fell slightly, realizing the miscommunication. "Hannah, I brought Mazie here for you as a gift. *She's* the surprise. She needs a loving home since her injury, and you... well," Niles scratched the back of his neck. "I thought maybe you could use some, er, company." His cheeks flushed slightly as he looked at Hannah.

Hannah's blue eyes went so wide she thought they might pop out of her head and she released a tiny squeak. "Gift? You want me to take Mazie... a dog?" She tilted her head and waited for his response.

As if on cue, Mazie jumped off of the porch swing, walked to Hannah's legs, and rubbed her snout against Hannah's legs before sitting proudly beside her.

Hannah felt something inside of her warm. She noted Mazie's wagging tail. *Mazie is more cheerful than the blue sky. She's ridiculously happy after having been shot. It was like Mazie didn't even remember it happened.*

Niles noticed the way Hannah looked at the dog and went in for the kill. "Look, why don't you just take her for a trial period. If things don't work out, you can give the lovely little Mazie back, no questions asked."

Hannah didn't object, so Niles continued. "Two weeks. Call it an experiment. Call it babysitting. Call it a sleepover! Whatever you want to call it, there's no pressure."

"Okay. Fine. Two weeks." Hannah's eyes met Niles'.

"Yeah! This is going to be great! You won't regret it. Mazie is the best, you two will be an amazing team."

Hannah reached down to pet Mazie.

"I need to get to work. Crime doesn't stop for any dog, right, Mazie?" Niles waved goodbye and headed to his shift as a state police officer. Hannah watched him leave with a mixture of pride; what a great guy her cousin was, and annoyance; what had her great cousin just gotten her into?

Hannah opened the door and Mazie obediently followed her inside. She crouched down and locked eyes with the dog. "A great team, huh? I wonder what sort of trouble you are going to get into?"

Mazie wagged her tail furiously, overjoyed to be with her new owner.

Hannah couldn't help but note Mazie's resilience, and despite herself, she found a smile crossing her own face.

Read the first 6 books.

Dog Detective – The Beagle Mysteries Book 1 to 6

ALSO BY ROSIE SAMS & AGATHA PARKER

To be the first to find out when Rosie & Agatha release a new book and to hear about other sweet romance authors join the exclusive SweetBookHub readers club here.

* * *

The Bakers and Bulldog Mysteries Collection – Grab all 20 books in this much loved series with the cutest French Bulldog Detective in all of Port Warren.

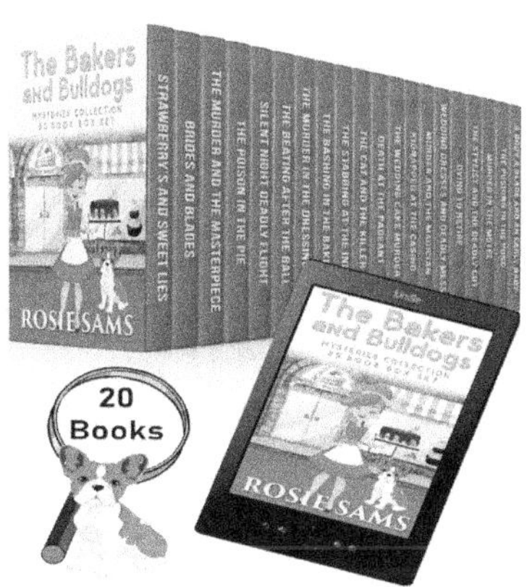

The Dog Detectives – The Beagle Mysteries

Sniffing out the Killer

On the Scent of Murder

Hunting Down the Heiress

Sweet Treats and Dirty Deeds

Retrieving the Clue

Decked to Death

Dragging Down the Culprit

Adding up to Murder

Murder for the Crafty Ladies and the Clever Beagle

The Art of Murder

If you enjoyed this book, Rosie and Agatha would appreciate it
if you left a review on Amazon or Goodreads

©Copyright 2021 Rosie Sams
All Rights Reserved
Rosie Sams

License Notes
This Book is licensed for personal enjoyment only. It may not be resold. Your continued respect for author's rights is appreciated.

This story is a work of fiction; any resemblance to people is purely coincidence. All places, names, events, businesses, etc. are used in a fictional manner. All characters are from the imagination of the author.

www.ingramcontent.com/pod-product-compliance
Lightning Source LLC
Chambersburg PA
CBHW071215130726
47998CB00002B/754